Published by Fledgling Press 2011
www.fledglingpress.co.uk

Printed and bound by Charlesworth Press

ISBN: 978-1-905916-28-3

Dedication

With Love and Thanks:
to Iona, for stealing her name,
and to Stuart,
without whom Peerie never would have found her magic.

N. x

Once upon a time, in a land that was very far away, there was a beautiful castle.
The outside of the castle was painted in all the colours of the rainbow, and each
room inside the castle was a different colour.
There was a red kitchen and a pink bathroom, a green library and a yellow hallway,
a purple attic and an orange staircase.

1

But the most important room of all belonged to the most important person of all.

Princess Iona loved all the colours of the rainbow, but her very favourite colour of all was a very special, very bright, very magical shade of blue.

This blue was so very special because it was
the colour of a very special eye.

And that eye belonged to a very special dog.

And that very special dog was the very hairy,
very muddy, very best friend of Princess Iona:
The Peerie Monster.

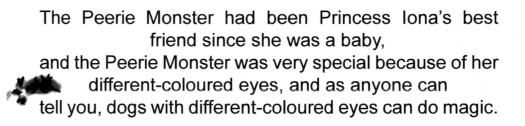

The Peerie Monster had been Princess Iona's best
friend since she was a baby,
and the Peerie Monster was very special because of her
different-coloured eyes, and as anyone can
tell you, dogs with different-coloured eyes can do magic.

Unfortunately, in the whole time that the Peerie Monster
had been living in the castle with Princess Iona, she had
never once shown any sign of having magical powers.

That didn't mean that she wasn't magic, just that she
was saving herself up for something really special.
Or so Princess Iona hoped.

Not that she would ever admit that to the Peerie Monster!

Princess Iona was a very good Princess, and the people loved her and her colourful castle.

However, on the other side of the forest there lived a wicked old witch who hated anything colourful.

She hated the many-coloured castle, and most of all she hated Princess Iona for always being so bright and cheerful.

She wanted the world to be black and white, and only on very special occasions would she allow a shade of grey.

One night, while Princess Iona and the Peerie Monster were asleep in the special blue bedroom, the wicked witch cast a spell.

It was a very dreadful spell. If Iona had looked out of her window, she would have seen birds and animals running out of the forest, to get as far away from the witch as possible.

But Iona was safely asleep so she did not look out of the window and did not see the birds or the animals. When she woke up she stretched, opened the curtains, and looked outside and saw a very dreadful thing indeed.

All the colours had gone.

The leaves were not green, and the sky was not blue.

She turned around and her very special blue bedroom was no longer a very special shade of blue.

It was grey.

The kitchen was grey and the bathroom was grey.

The library and the hallway, the attic and the stairs were all grey.

The walls of the castle were grey.

Everything as far as the eye could see was grey.

But worst of all, when Iona ran crying to the Peerie Monster and picked her up, both of Peerie's eyes were exactly the same shade of dismal grey!

This was more than poor Iona could take, and she threw herself down on her grey bed and sobbed and sobbed and sobbed until she could sob no more.

The Peerie Monster had watched Iona running around the castle, and she had looked outside, and she had seen the dismal grey. When she saw Iona so upset, she made a decision.

The Peerie Monster decided that she would have to Do Something.
Even if she wasn't entirely sure what that Something might be.

Creeping carefully out of Princess Iona's dismal grey bedroom, down the dismal grey stairs and out of the dismal grey front door, the Peerie Monster sat down on the dismal grey lawn, and thought.

The Peerie Monster was not used to thinking very often, and it made her head feel funny. But she thought, and she thought, and, as she thought, she felt a strange sensation at the bottom of her ears, and at the curl of her tail.

And most of all, she felt a strange sensation, right at the tips of her hairy little toes.

And that sensation made her want to walk. The Peerie Monster didn't know where she was walking to, but she kept on going, trusting that her toes would take her there, eventually.

She walked through the dismal grey woods, past the dismal grey flowers, and across the dismal grey stream, and then the Peerie Monster began to worry.

What would happen if her hairy little toes didn't take her to the right place?

The Peerie Monster walked and walked, and eventually she came to a big clearing. In the clearing was a pond, and next to the pond was the biggest crocodile the Peerie Monster had ever seen.

And the crocodile was crying.

Now, it is a well known fact that most crocodiles will eat a Peerie Monster for breakfast and still have room left over for some cake, but this crocodile looked so very sad that the Peerie Monster didn't feel afraid.

The Peerie Monster carefully crept up to the crocodile and coughed, quietly, so as not to alarm him.

The crocodile looked at the Peerie Monster, and the Peerie Monster looked at the crocodile. They sat, and they looked at each other, and just when the Peerie Monster was starting to worry that maybe she was going to be eaten, the crocodile spoke.

"Why aren't you afraid of me?" the crocodile said, in a very deep, very woeful voice. "Crocodiles eat Peerie Monsters for breakfast, you know."

The Peerie Monster was not afraid so she explained all about poor Princess Iona, and how her toes had brought her here, and how the crocodile had looked so sad, and was there anything that she could do to help?

The crocodile was surprised, for not many people care if a crocodile is happy or not, and he told the Peerie Monster that he was crying because of the witch's spell too.

For this was no ordinary crocodile. This was the Colour Crocodile, the Keeper of the Rainbow. To make all the colours in the world vanish, the wicked witch had stolen the scales of the Colour Crocodile, and until they were found there would be no more rainbows.

And without rainbows, the world would stay a dismal grey forever.

The Colour Crocodile explained that the only way to bring back the colours was to find his scales, one in each colour of the rainbow. If they were planted in the ground they would grow into a rainbow.

The crocodile said it would not be easy to find his scales. The wicked witch had probably destroyed most of them. But he was sure that one of each colour would be hiding from the witch.

The Peerie Monster was not a very big dog, or a very clever dog, but she was a very brave dog, and she loved Princess Iona very, very much.

And so the Peerie Monster made another Decision: she was going to find the scales, bring the rainbows back and make Princess Iona happy again.

The Peerie Monster thanked the Colour Crocodile very politely for not eating her, and set off back through the forest.

She did not know where she was going to find the scales, but the tips of her hairy little toes were tingling again, and that was good enough for now.

The Peerie Monster at first ambled cheerfully through the dismal grey forest, but then she started thinking.

The Peerie Monster was not a good thinker, and thinking twice in such a short space of time was definitely an alarming sign that something was very wrong with the world.

The Peerie Monster was thinking about where she might find the Colour Scales.

Would they be hidden away up high?

Would they be hidden away in the sea?

Would they be disguised as something else?

Would they be hidden away under things?

The Peerie Monster was not a very big dog,
and she could not reach very high.

The Peerie Monster was very hairy, and so she sank more often than she swam.

The Peerie Monster was not very clever,
and was not very good as seeing through disguises.
The Peerie Monster decided that the best she could hope for was that the scales were hidden
under things, for she was a very good digger.

And, if they were hidden in mud then that would be very fabulous indeed.

Then the Peerie Monster had her very biggest, most worrying thought. It was such a big, worrying thought that she stopped and sat down immediately.

What if . . . all the Colour Crocodile's scales had turned a dismal grey too? How on earth would she know what they were? How would she know if she had all the colours?

Suddenly everything was looking a lot more difficult, and the Peerie Monster started to think, for the very first time, that maybe, just maybe, she might not be able to bring back the rainbows and make Princess Iona happy again.

The Peerie Monster was extremely upset at this very worrying thought, and she lay down in the middle of the path, laid her head on her paws and looked around the forest.

The forest seemed very, very big, and the Peerie Monster felt very, very small, and more than a little bit lonely, all by herself in the forest.

Just as she was about to start crying, the wind blew through the trees and something caught her eye.

The Peerie Monster jumped up and looked harder.

Carefully and quietly, she began to creep through the trees, all the time never looking away, not even blinking.

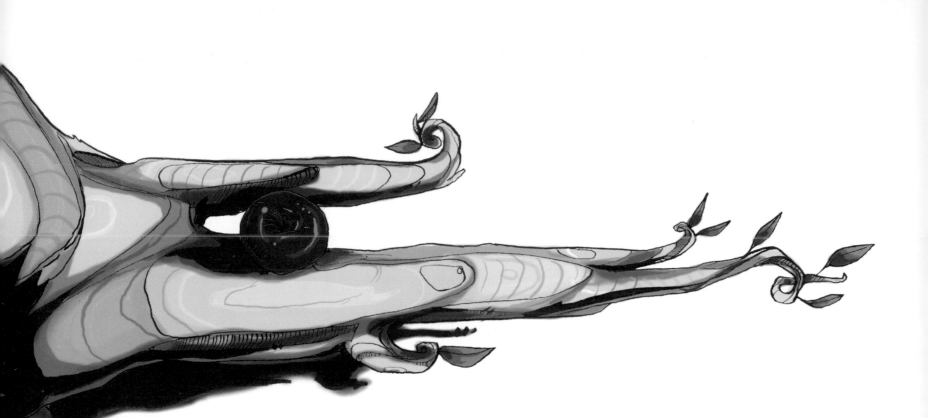

For there, through the trees, up in the highest of the high branches on the tallest of the tall trees, was an apple. And the apple was a bright, beautiful shade of red!

The Peerie Monster was very excited!

Not everything in the world had turned a dismal grey – there was still one bit of colour left at least.

And then the Peerie Monster had a thought.

What if this apple was one of the scales of the Colour Crocodile? How would she get it down?
She was only a little dog, and the tree was very tall.

She would need to climb.

As the Peerie Monster thought about how to climb the tree, she felt a strange tickling in her hairy little toes. The feeling got stronger and stronger, and soon she was wriggling around to try and make it stop. And then, peeking through her rather long, rather muddy fur, she saw her claws.

Somehow, they had grown very long and very sharp.

The Peerie Monster very carefully put one front paw on the tree trunk, and then the other one. And her claws sank through the bark and gripped on.

Then the Peerie Monster very carefully put one back paw on the tree trunk, and then the other one.

Very slowly, and very carefully, the Peerie Monster began to climb the tree. She had been climbing for at least ten minutes when she looked to see how high up she was.

That was a mistake. Peerie Monsters do not like heights, and this Peerie Monster had climbed very high indeed.

She stopped climbing and gulped. Her legs started to shake, and her tail started to shake. Her ears and her nose and even her hairy little toes, started to shake. As she shook, she could feel her long, pointy claws loosening from the bark, and the Peerie Monster got very worried indeed.

She took one last look at the ground and looked back up at the apple again. And she realised that she could reach the beautiful, bright red apple if she just took one paw off the tree trunk.

The Peerie Monster was very frightened, but she was a very brave little dog, and she knew that she had to at least try and reach the apple.

Slowly and carefully, she reached out with one paw and snagged the apple on one of her long pointy claws.

Slowly and carefully she put the apple into her mouth, and slowly and carefully she began to climb back down the tree, making sure that she didn't look down.

The Peerie Monster finally made it all the way down and as soon as she had all four paws back on the ground her hairy little toes started to tickle once more, and the next thing she knew her claws had shrunk back to their normal size.

Once she had stopped staring at her feet, wondering how on earth her claws had done that, she turned her attention to the apple. However, it was an apple no longer. It was now a very red, very shiny crocodile scale!

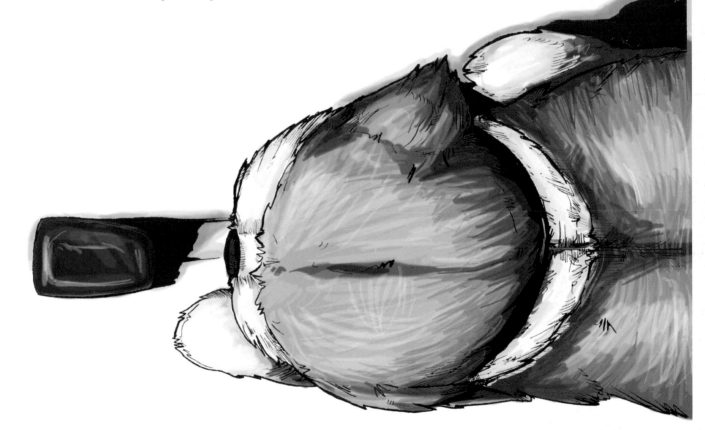

The Peerie Monster had done it! She had found the first scale!

The Peerie Monster was so excited and pleased with herself that she did a little dance and then was just so very excited that she had to roll around on her back for a little while with a big smile on her face!

She eventually decided that enough was enough, carefully tucked the scale into her collar, and set off again, once more following the tingling in her hairy little toes.

Far away from the Peerie Monster, in a dismal grey kitchen in a dismal grey castle, right at the back of a shelf, a teapot suddenly turned a bright, beautiful shade of red.

But there was no-one around to see it.

Princess Iona was still crying in her dismal grey bedroom, and everyone else had run away like the animals and birds, to try and find somewhere where there were still colours.

The Peerie Monster followed her hairy little toes, and soon she had found an orange snail shell hidden under a log . . .

. . . a green feather which fell out of a bird's wing . . .

. . . and a bright yellow daffodil waving by the river bank.

And back in the dismal grey castle, one by one, an orange stair . . .

. . . one green book . . .

. . . and a yellow lampshade had appeared.

But there was still no one to see them.

By now, the Peerie Monster was feeling very pleased with herself indeed, and she was thinking that she might just make it back to the castle in time for a nice cup of hot chocolate before bed time. There was just one colour left ... purple.

But though the Peerie Monster searched high, and though the Peerie Monster searched low, she saw no trace of purple anywhere.

And the whole time it was getting darker and darker, and the shadows were getting longer and longer, and the Peerie Monster was getting more and more worried.

Finally, the Peerie Monster realised that she would not make it back to the castle in time for hot chocolate with Iona. In fact, she wouldn't even make it back to the castle in time for bed.

She would have to sleep in the forest!

The Peerie Monster was a very brave little dog, but she had never slept in the forest before, especially not on her own. And she had heard all sorts of horrid stories about Big and Scary Monsters who lived in the forest, and who would not be nice to little Peerie Monsters.

And so it was a very scared little Peerie Monster who finally curled up for the night in a big pile of leaves, hidden under a big rock. She tried and she tried to fall asleep, for she was very tired, but every time she heard a noise in the forest she would jump awake and look around, in case there was a monster nearby.

The sixteenth time this happened, the Peerie Monster noticed a very strange shadow.

It was the shadow of the rock she was hiding under, and unlike all the other shadows around her, this one was not a dismal grey colour.

This shadow was purple!

The Peerie Monster was very excited at finding the last colour, but she was also very confused. How can you pick up a shadow?

As she sat and thought and thought, the Peerie Monster felt a very strange sensation. In fact, it was the same strange sensation that she had felt when her claws had grown so very long and pointy to help her climb the tree.

But this time, the sensation was in her very long, very hairy tail.

As she stared at it, the Peerie Monster's tail changed. The Peerie Monster was very proud of her tail, for it was very hairy, and very silky, and it was so very long that she could, if she wanted, wrap it right around her neck like a scarf!

But now, her tail was becoming bushy, and the hairs were no longer silky but stiff and wiry, and soon her tail looked almost exactly like a big sweeping brush.

And that was when the Peerie Monster had an idea.

Creeping very carefully and quietly up to the purple shadow, so as not to frighten it, the Peerie Monster suddenly turned around and with one mighty swoosh of her tail, swept up the shadow and caught in her paws!

As soon as it was caught, the shadow quietly and peacefully turned back into a beautiful colourful crocodile scale. And back at the dismal grey castle, one curtain in the attic turned purple.

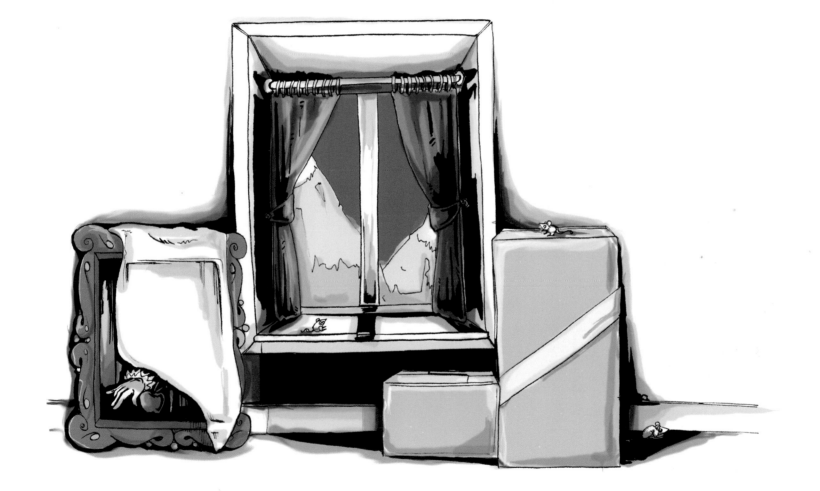

But there was still no one around to see it.

The Peerie Monster was so excited that she forgot all about being afraid of the dark, and she set off running to the castle.

She ran and ran, and just when she thought her little legs could not run any more, there it was.

There, just appearing out of the mist, lit up by the dismal grey rays of the rising, dismal, grey sun, was the dismal grey castle. And right at the very top, the Peerie Monster could just make out one purple curtain waving in the breeze, as if to welcome her home.

And she knew that her plan had worked.

The Peerie Monster skipped through the dismal grey gardens until she was right outside Princess Iona's bedroom window. And there, right in the middle of the flower beds, exactly where she had never been allowed to dig before, the Peerie Monster did what Peerie Monsters do best: she dug a hole!

She dug and she dug and she dug until she was covered from head to toe in dismal grey mud. And then, with a huge grin on her very dirty face, she very carefully put the scales of the Colour Crocodile into the hole.

Very carefully, the Peerie Monster covered the scales back up, and then she sat and she waited.

And she waited. And she waited some more.

But nothing happened. No rainbow. No colours. Not even a single blade of grass or a petal on a flower changed from dismal grey.

While she waited, the Peerie Monster heard Princess Iona's window open above her.

The Peerie Monster was about to bark to tell Iona that she was back, when she heard Iona cry.

"It's still so dismally grey. And the Peerie Monster has run away from me, I just can't bear it!" she cried, before slamming the window shut and going back to hide in her dismal grey bed.

And then the Peerie Monster realised why there was no rainbow. She had not collected all the colours. There was still one missing, and it was the most important one.

She had not collected a scale in the very special, very magical shade of blue that exactly matched the colour of her very special, very magical eye.

And with that, the Peerie Monster started to cry.

She cried, and she cried, and she cried so hard that she did not even notice that one of the tears rolling down her very hairy, very dirty nose was a very special colour indeed.

This tear had come from a very special, very magical eye, and when it hit the ground at the Peerie Monster's feet, it changed from a tear into a giant, glittering scale.

As soon as the scale hit the ground there was a terrific rumbling sound from underneath the Peerie Monster's very hairy toes, and right in front of her very hairy nose a huge, brightly coloured rainbow erupted out of the earth, soaring high into the sky, over the castle and the lawn, over the woods and away over the horizon.

As the rainbow travelled across the sky, colours started to appear, slowly at first but quicker and quicker, until it was as if someone was throwing giant pots of paint around!

The Peerie Monster was so happy that she stopped her crying and started to bark and bark and bark from sheer joy.

Princess Iona heard her barking and came out from under her very special blue duvet.

She saw that her room was once more a very special shade of blue and, running down the orange stairs and across the yellow hall, she threw open the rainbow door and saw ... everything!

All the colours were back!

Right outside of her window was a giant rainbow, and at the foot of the rainbow was a very hairy, very dirty, very wonderful little dog, with one brown eye and one very special, very magical blue eye.

Princess Iona and the Peerie Monster were delighted to see each other, and Princess Iona didn't even care that her flower bed was ruined, or that there was mud everywhere.

A large, many-coloured crocodile watched the very hairy, very muddy little dog from the edge of the forest. He smiled a very crocodile smile, and went to pay a visit to a certain witch he knew; a witch whose howls of frustration he had heard echoing across the forest.

Princess Iona and the Peerie Monster were so happy they didn't notice the crocodile. Nor did they ever realise that it's true what they say about dogs with different-coloured eyes:

They can do magic.